The Mystery Mess

written by Billy Aronson

illustrated by Shari Warren

**McGraw-Hill
School Division**

New York   Farmington

"You've got to believe me," Carlos
begged his Aunt Sara. "I didn't make this
mess!"

Carlos had been enjoying his week
visiting his aunt. He loved playing in her
living room, where he would draw and
play games. But his favorite thing to do
was to make buildings out of blocks. His
buildings were very tall and beautiful.

Carlos always cleaned up the living room before he went to bed. But every morning, to his surprise, it was a mess again.

"I'm not angry," Aunt Sara said. "But if you have to get up early in the morning and play, please put the toys away."

"I don't get up early and play!" Carlos
said.

"You can't argue with the facts," his
aunt explained. "You and I are the only
ones here. And I don't get up that early.
So it must be you."

"What about Raphael?" asked Carlos.

"Raphael?" She laughed. "That cat's too lazy to make such a big mess. He sleeps most of the day. Every night he curls up on your bed. And every morning he's still there, in the exact same spot."

Aunt Sara was right about the cat
being lazy. But Carlos still wasn't certain.

"I'm pretty sure you're making the
mess," he told Raphael. "But how can I
catch you at it? I'd sit up and watch you
all night . . . but I'd fall asleep."

As Carlos tried to think of a plan, the phone rang.

Suddenly, he had an idea. He asked Aunt Sara if he could walk to the pet store on the corner.

"Raphael needs a new collar," he explained, smiling.

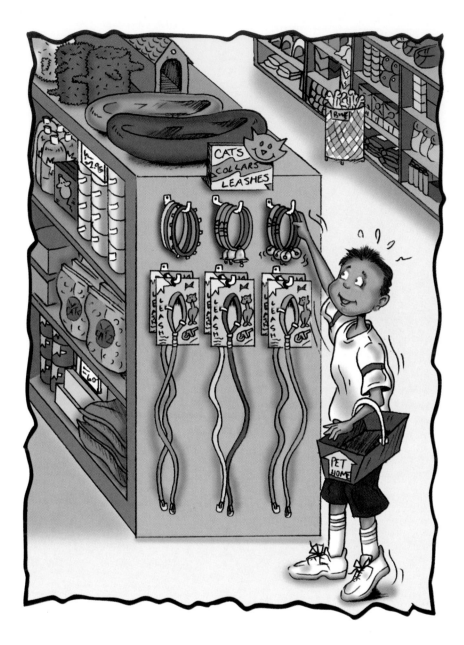

At the pet store, there were several neat things to explore. But Carlos knew exactly what he wanted.

That night, before he went to bed, Carlos tried out the new collar. He slipped it around Raphael's neck.

"This better work, Raphael," Carlos said. Raphael purred and jumped into Carlos's lap. The bells on the collar jingled noisily.

Early the next morning, Carlos woke
up to the sound of bells. He looked
around his room for Raphael. The cat was
nowhere to be found. Then he heard
jingling coming from the hall.

Carlos hurried along in search of
Raphael. The cat wasn't in the hall. He
wasn't in the kitchen. Carlos could hear
the bells, but he couldn't find Raphael!

Then Carlos smiled. He knew exactly where he could find Raphael! He tiptoed into the living room. He peeked around the door.

There, in the early morning light, he saw Raphael. But Raphael wasn't acting lazy at all! He was more like a tiger, out in the wilds of nature! He jumped on toys. He scratched at paper. He fought with crayons. He attacked every object like it was another animal. The bells on his collar jingled loudly.

"I can hardly believe this," thought Carlos. "And Aunt Sara will never believe it. How will I be able to prove it?

"I could go wake her up. But I don't want to disturb her so early in the morning."

Suddenly, Aunt Sara was standing
next to Carlos. She had been awakened
by the noisy jingling of the bells.

"Aha!" she exclaimed. "Now I know you
get up in the morning and make a mess."

"I didn't make the mess," said Carlos,
pointing toward the cat. "It was Raphael!"

"Who?" asked Aunt Sara. Raphael was
nowhere to be seen.

Just then they heard bells. Raphael jumped up from behind the couch. He leaped into the air and landed on top of Carlos's building. Blocks went tumbling all over the room. What a mess!

Carlos turned to his aunt. She was laughing and shaking her head.

"Like you told me, Aunt Sara," said Carlos, "You can't argue with the facts!"